BOOMA

BOOMA

BOOMA

BOOM

For Mom and Dad—GS

For my brave nephew, Lucas—LF

Magination Press
Books for Kids From the
American Psychological Association
maginationpress.org

Book design by Rachel Ross
Printed by Phoenix Color, Hagerstown, MD

Library of Congress Cataloging-in-Publication Data
Names: Silver, Gail, author. | Fields, Lisa, illustrator.
Title: Booma booma boom/by Gail Silver ; illustrated by Lisa Fields.
Description: Washington : Magination Press, 2022. | Summary: A courageous boy emerges from under his bed to guide his stuffed animal companions through a thunderstorm.
Identifiers: LCCN 2021036180 (print) | LCCN 2021036181 (ebook) | ISBN 9781433837012 (hardcover) | ISBN 9781433837029 (ebook)
Subjects: LCSH: Thunderstorms—Juvenile fiction. | Thunder—Juvenile fiction. | Fear—Juvenile fiction. | Courage—Juvenile fiction. | CYAC: Stories in rhyme. | Thunder—Fiction. | Thunderstorms—Fiction. | Fear—Fiction. | LCGFT: Stories in rhyme. | Picture books.
Classification: LCC PZ8.3.S58412 Bo 2022 (print) | LCC PZ8.3.S58412 (ebook) | DDC [E]—dc23
LC record available at https://lccn.loc.gov/2021036180
LC ebook record available at https://lccn.loc.gov/2021036181

Manufactured in the United States of America
10 9 8 7 6 5 4 3 2 1

BOOMA BOOMA Boom

By Gail Silver
Illustrated by
Lisa Fields

Magination Press • Washington, DC
American Psychological Association

BOOM

The thunder has arrived. I think it's in my room.

Teddy, Bess, and Fred are trying to be brave,
pretending they're not scared
each time thunder waves.

They're waiting for a rescue
on this loud and rainy night.

It's up to me to navigate
the sudden flashing light.

I'll hug them close and hold them tight
and once we're all together
I think they'll feel alright.

I'll tell them plain and simple:

"For what it might be worth, thunder's just the clouds talking to the earth."

Okay, well yeah, the storm is kind of loud,
but its rain grows trees and plants
which bring us food and fruit,
and cotton for our pants.

We can huddle under cover
and watch the drops of water
race across the glass.

We'll guess which one is slowest
and sure to finish last.

Then we'll close our eyes and listen
to the wash of falling rain.
It's sort of kind of soothing
as it cleans the windowpane.

It's not the thunder that's so scary,
just the way that it arrives.
It comes without a warning,
and takes us by surprise.

So let's cuddle up and listen
to the rumble n' the rain.
And tell Fred that he'll feel better
brushing Bessie's mane.
We'll count each stroke together
'til Bess is fully groomed.
And start again at "one"
each time the sky goes...

BOOMA BOOMA BOOMA BOOM

Three...

With every stroke, we breathe.
We brush Bessie from above,
and then from underneath.

"Four n' five...
Six n' seven..."

Mama pokes her head in,
and so I say to come in.
"You can help us groom.
We start again at 'one'
each time the sky goes..."

BOOMA BOOMA BOOM

"One...

Two...

Three..."

With each stroke, we breathe.
We brush Bessie from above,
and then from underneath.

"Four n' five...
Six n' seven..."

Papa pops his head in,
and so I say to come in.
"You can help us groom.
We start again at 'one'
each time the sky goes..."

BOOMA BOOMA BOOM

"One...
Two...
Three..."

With each stroke, we breathe.
We brush Bessie from above,
and then from underneath.

"Four n' five...
Six n' seven..."

Bessie's getting tired.
So are Ted and Fred.
They say they want to sleep
beside me in my bed.

They take a stretch and yawn a breath,
then rest on top of me.
They're floating up and down.
They feel my belly breathe.

I think I'm kind of tired.
I yawn into my sleeve.

I rest my head on Mama.
I can feel her breathe.

Mama's kind of tired.
She yawns into her sleeve.
She rests her head on Papa,
who's fallen fast asleep—
except his lips are moving.
He's talking as he breathes.

I close my eyes and listen.
It's so quiet I can hear him.

I know the words. I know their rhythm.
I know them well, and so I say them.

"For what it might be worth...
thunder's just the clouds
talking to the earth.

Thunder's just the clouds
talking to the earth.

Thunder's just the clouds
talking to the earth..."

BOOMA BOOMA Boom

Reader's Note

by Julia Martin Burch, PhD

Most children experience fears at various points in childhood. Thinking back, you can likely recall something you were afraid of as a child! Children typically outgrow their fears as they get older and mature; however, coping with fears can be very challenging in the moment. Storms are a very common childhood fear. They are loud, unpredictable, and out of human control, which can feel very scary to children. The following are some tips for parents to support a young child who is afraid of storms.

Validate Their Emotions

Let your child know that it's okay that they feel afraid of thunderstorms. Well-intended parents sometimes minimize a child's fear in hopes that the child will stop worrying ("it's nothing to be scared of"), but dismissing an emotion tends to have the opposite effect. The child does not feel heard or taken seriously and as a result, often has an even bigger emotional reaction. Instead, it is helpful to say something like "I understand that you feel very scared when you hear thunder" or "you're really worried about a storm coming tonight." By communicating that you understand that your child is afraid, you help them feel heard, which is soothing.

Teach your child that it is normal to feel afraid at times. If you have an age-appropriate example of something you were afraid of as a child, consider sharing it. It can also be helpful to discuss characters in movies or books who have fears.

Educate

Share age-appropriate information about storms with your child. For example, in the story, the main character reminds himself that rain helps plants grow and that thunder isn't dangerous, but is just surprising when it arrives suddenly. Consider sharing other interesting storm facts, such as that thunder is the sound caused by lightning or that light travels faster than sound, so we see lightning before we hear thunder. It is helpful to adapt explanations to your child's level of understanding. For example, for younger children you might use the main character's explanation of storms as "thunder is clouds talking to the earth." It's also helpful to make the discussions fun. You might compare lightning to fireworks or a light show or recreate thunder noises with pots and pans.

Teach Your Child to Self-Soothe

Kids feel more confident facing fears when they know how to calm themselves down. Teach your child how to soothe themselves in scary moments. Focusing on a particular sense and engaging in a pleasant activity using that sense is a great place to start. In the story, the main character soothes himself with his sense of touch by grooming his stuffed horse and hugging his other stuffed animals. Have fun with your child practicing a range of self-soothing strategies focused on different senses to see what helps them feel calm. For example, they might look at pictures of loved ones or a fun vacation, listen to a calming song or white noise machine, smell a comforting object or scented lotion, or focus on a cool drink of water. Coach them to fully focus on the sense and how the activity makes them feel while they try it. Get curious afterwards about which helped them feel the most calm.

It can also be helpful to mindfully focus on one thing in the environment, such as watching the raindrops as the character does in the story. Try to make this activity game-like, for example guessing which raindrop will reach the bottom of the pane first. Another example of a game-like mindfulness activity is counting as many objects of a certain shape or color as you can find in the space around you.

Finally, teach your child to take slow, calming breaths into their belly when they are afraid. A fun and effective way to teach this skill is by putting a stuffed animal on your child's belly and having them raise it up and down with their breath. It is also helpful to breathe in for slightly less time than they breathe out. For example, have your child count slowly to two while they breathe in and raise the stuffed animal, and out for three while they breathe out and lower the stuffed animal.

No matter which strategies you teach your child, it is best to teach them for the first time in a calm moment (i.e., not in the middle of a thunderstorm!). Practice the strategies often with your child so that they are very familiar with them and can call on them easily in an anxious moment. Praise your child and express how proud you are of them for working to calm down whenever they try a self-soothing skill, even if they say it does not work. Any practice is a step towards a new, calmer response to storms and will pay off in the long run.

Model Calm and Confidence

As a parent, it can be incredibly difficult to see your child upset. Parents naturally want to comfort their child in whatever way will work best in the moment. Yet coping with worries about storms are actually a wonderful opportunity for your child to learn important emotion-regulation skills and to practice being brave and calm in the face of a stressor. During a storm, strive to find a balance between comforting and reassuring your child and communicating confidence that they can handle this scary situation with independence. For example, you might say "I know you're feeling really nervous about the thunder, and I also know you are brave and can handle this. Let's do a few belly breaths together and then you can keep doing them on your own after I leave your room." Model the calm you would like to see from your child.

Do your best not to allow your child to rely solely on your presence for comfort and reassurance. The father in the story accidentally falls briefly asleep in the main character's bed during the storm, but the parents are not planning to stay in their son's room. Though allowing your child to sleep with you can be a very tempting solution (and sometimes hard to avoid as a tired parent!), do your best to not make it a habit. This is important because, when your child shares a bed with you due to fear, they learn this is the best way to handle worries, which can be a very slippery slope. They also do not get the chance to learn that they are brave and capable of facing fears themselves. The parents in the story come in to check on the child, but they let him lead with his own self-soothing strategies, and after a few minutes they will return to their own room.

When to Seek Support

As mentioned previously, it is normal for children to experience a variety of fears at different points during childhood. However, if your child's fear is so intense or distressing that it impacts their functioning (for example, they are so afraid of bees, they will not play outside), consider consulting with a licensed mental health professional who specializes in cognitive behavioral therapy, and particularly, exposure and response prevention (ERP) treatment. ERP is a highly effective, research-supported treatment for intense fears in children.

Julia Martin Burch, PhD, is a staff psychologist at the McLean Anxiety Mastery Program at McLean Hospital in Boston. Dr. Martin Burch completed her training at Fairleigh Dickinson University and Massachusetts General Hospital/Harvard Medical School. She works with children, teens, and parents and specializes in cognitive behavioral therapy for anxiety, obsessive-compulsive disorder, and related disorders. Outside of her work at McLean, Dr. Martin Burch gives talks to clinicians, parent groups, and schools on working with anxious youth.

Gail Silver, JD, E-RYT, RCYT, is an award-winning author and contributor to *Lions Roar Magazine*. Gail travels nationally and internationally to facilitate mindfulness-based education. She is the Founder and Director of Yoga Child Inc. and the Founder and CEO of The School Mindfulness Project. She lives in Philadelphia, PA.

Visit gailsilver.com, @AuthorGailSilver on Facebook, @GailPSilver on Twitter, and @GailSilver1 on Instagram.

Lisa Fields received her BFA in Illustration from Ringling College of Art and Design. Lisa is also a member of the Society of Children's Book Writers and Illustrators. She lives in New York.

Visit lisafields.com, @LisaFieldsIllustration on Facebook, and @LisaFieldsIll on Twitter and Instagram.

Magination Press is the children's book imprint of the American Psychological Association. APA works to advance psychology as a science and profession and as a means of promoting health and human welfare. Magination Press books reach young readers and their parents and caregivers to make navigating life's challenges a little easier. It's the combined power of psychology and literature that makes a Magination Press book special.

Visit maginationpress.org and @MaginationPress on Facebook, Twitter, Instagram, and Pinterest.